P9-DNK-689

BAD KITTY

★ VS ★

UNCLE MURRAY

NICK BRUEL

BAD KITTY

★ VS ★

UNCLE MURRAY

THE UPROAR AT THE FRONT DOOR

SCHOLASTIC INC.
New York Toronto London Auckland
Sydney Mexico City New Delhi Hong Kong

No part of this publication may be reproduced, stored in a
retrieval system, or transmitted in any form or by any means, electronic,
mechanical, photocopying, recording, or otherwise, without written permission
of the publisher. For information regarding permission, write to Roaring Brook
Press, a division of Holtzbrinck Publishing Holdings Limited Partnership,
175 Fifth Avenue, New York, NY 10010.

ISBN 978-0-545-28919-1

Copyright © 2010 by Nick Bruel. All rights reserved.
Published by Scholastic Inc., 557 Broadway, New York, NY 10012, by
arrangement with Roaring Brook Press, a division of Holtzbrinck Publishing
Holdings Limited Partnership. SCHOLASTIC and associated logos are
trademarks and/or registered trademarks of Scholastic Inc.

12 11 10 9 8 7 6 5 4 3 2 1   10 11 12 13 14 15/0

Printed in the U.S.A.   40

First Scholastic printing, September 2010

To Neal

• CONTENTS •

❖ CONTENTS ❖

•CHAPTER ONE•

PUSSYCAT
PARADISE

WELCOME, KITTY!

Welcome to Pussycat Paradise, where everything you see is made entirely out of **FOOD**—food for your belly!

The mountains are made out of kibble. The trees are made out of sausages and bacon. Cans of cat food grow out of the ground. And the grass is made out of catnip.

Yes, Kitty! Eat! EAT! Food is everywhere! The rocks are made out of turkey and giblets. The dirt is made out of tuna fish. Even the rivers flow with beef gravy.

And the best part, of course, is that YOU are the only one here! No dogs to hound you. No people to make you take a bath. There is no one else here. Only you.

Be careful, Kitty. Don't touch that can. It's the only thing holding up that gigantic chicken liver.

OH NO! TOO LATE! The gigantic chicken liver is going to fall! Look out, Kitty! LOOK OUT!!

WHOOPS!

Sorry, Kitty. I hope I didn't wake you when I dropped the suitcase.

That's right, Kitty. We're going on a little trip. We'll be gone for a while.

Sorry, Kitty. You're not going with us. You'll have to stay home with Puppy.

Oh, don't be like that, Kitty. We'll be back in just a week. And when we get back, we'll have a REALLY BIG SURPRISE for you!

That's right, Kitty. **A REALLY BIG SURPRISE!** You like surprises, don't you?

In the meantime, Kitty, you won't be alone. We found someone who's going to stay here and feed you and take good care of you and Puppy while we're gone.

In fact, that must be him!

Where did Kitty go? Oh, well. At least Puppy is excited to see who's here.

25

There you are, Kitty. Don't you want to say "Hi" to good ol' Uncle Murray?

Awww! You're a good dog, aren't you?

UNCLE MURRAY'S FUN FACTS

WHY ARE SOME CATS AFRAID OF PEOPLE?

I was just wondering about that.

No one ever talks about a "scaredy-giraffe" or a "scaredy-penguin" or even a "scaredy-dog," but everyone's heard of "scaredy-cats"! That's because cats use fear as a very valuable tool for survival.

The average weight for a cat is only around 10 pounds. Imagine what your life would be like if you lived with someone who was almost TWENTY TIMES BIGGER than you! That's what life is like for a cat living with a human being. Having good reflexes to avoid being stepped on or sat upon is very important.

CAT: AROUND 10 POUNDS.

BIG, FAT, GOOFY-LOOKING AUTHOR OF THIS BOOK: 185 POUNDS.

REALLY? DOES THIS BOOK MAKE ME LOOK FAT?

But sometimes a cat's fear of people can become exaggerated. Sometimes this happens when a kitten is raised without any human contact. It can also happen if a cat or a kitten has had a bad experience with a person.

But I'm a nice guy! I wouldn't hurt a fly, much less a dog or a cat, no matter how goofy it is.

It doesn't matter. A cat's instinct always tells her to be careful around people, especially strangers. The best way to get a cat to grow used to you is to be patient, be gentle, be quiet, and try not to take the cat's reaction to you too personally.

And one more thing . . . Try not to make any sudden, loud noises. Cats hate that.

No loud, sudden noises. Got it! What kind of jerk do you think I am? Everybody knows that!

Bye, Uncle Murray! Thank you for taking care of Kitty and Puppy while we're gone. We'll see you in a week!

By the way, you have to really push hard on this door to close it. If you don't, it won't really shut properly.

Okey doke! Goodbye! Good luck!

•CHAPTER TWO•
HIDE!

HOLY SALAMI! That goofy cat's just making things worse and worse!

I see you there pretending to be a dishrag again, ya goofy cat! Don't scream at me. Don't scream at me. Don't scream at me. Don't scream at me. Don't scream at me. Don't scream at me . . .

All I really wanted was to sit down, relax, have some lunch, and maybe watch a little TV.

All I really wanted was to sit down, relax, have some lunch, and maybe watch a little TV.

All I really wanted was to sit down, relax, have some lunch, and maybe watch a little TV.

All I really wanted was to sit down, relax, have some lunch, and maybe watch a little TV.

•CHAPTER THREE•
THE KITTY DIARIES

64

•CHAPTER FOUR•

UNCLE MURRAY
STRIKES BACK

Y'know, . . . this
stuff doesn't
look half bad.

KITTY PUPPY

Y'know, dog . . . when I was just a kid, I had a pooch a lot like you. He was a good dog, too.

I named him Sam, and I found him lost and hungry in an alley near where I lived. He was all white except for some black spots on his face and one of his back legs.

Anyways, I still had half a sandwich on me from lunch so I tossed it to him. Boy, oh, boy was he happy to get some food into his little dog belly. You'd think he hadn't eaten anything in a year. It was just baloney, after all. No mustard, even.

I used my belt as a leash and put it around Sam's neck. At first I thought he'd go crazy when I started to pull him, but he didn't. In fact, he barked and licked my hand the whole way home.

But there was a problem. My mother wouldn't let me keep Sam in the house 'cause my baby sister was real allergic to dogs. I guess it was true, 'cause she still is. I told my mom I would keep Sam only in my room, but she told me that wouldn't really work. She was right.

So I did the only thing I could think of . . . I took little Sam to a dog shelter where they'd feed him and take good care of him.

They were real nice to Sam there. He had his own little cage, and there were lots of other dogs there for him to talk to. But the best part was that they said I could come visit him every day after school. So I did!

I went to visit Sam every single day, and each time he saw me he'd jump up and lick my face and wrestle me to the ground like he was sayin' "Gee, I'm really happy to see you! Where've you been?"

Each day, I taught him a new trick. I taught him to sit and to stay. I taught him to beg and to roll over. I even taught him geography. NAHHH! I'm just kidding about that last one. But he really was smart.

Gee, Sam and I had a lot of fun together.Then one day I walked in and didn't see him there.

K-CHOO!

A lady who worked at the shelter told me a family had come in just after I left the day before, fell in love with Sam, and took him home. She said they were real nice people and promised to feed him and take good care of him. But that didn't help. I started crying like Niagara Falls. He may not have lived with me, but Sam was <u>MY</u> <u>DOG</u>!

I thought for sure that I'd never see little Sam again.

But then, one day, about a year later, as I was walking through the park, I looked over and saw a little girl playing with a dog that looked a whole lot like my Sam. He was all white except for some black spots on his face and one of his back legs. It <u>was</u> him! And they were having a swell time. Sam was even doing some of the same tricks that <u>I</u> taught him.

It hurt me so much inside to see this little girl playing with my dog. <u>MY DOG</u>. But then I looked at how much fun they were having and how happy he looked, and I thought to myself . . . all I ever really wanted for that lost, hungry dog sitting alone in that alley was for someone to take him home and feed him and take good care of him. Right? And that's what I got.

I loved that dog, and now I knew that someone else loved that dog as much as me.

It was one of those days that was both real good and real bad at the same time.

SNIFFLE

81

UNCLE MURRAY'S FUN FACTS

WHY ARE CATS AFRAID OF VACUUM CLEANERS?

It's not the vacuum cleaner that frightens cats so much as the sudden, loud noise it makes. Most cats will react quickly to any sudden, loud noise like a car horn, or a firecracker, or someone yelling.

Cats can hear very, very well—even better than dogs. In fact, a cat can hear three times better than a human being. That's why a cat can hear a mouse rustling through the grass from 30 feet away. But it's also why loud noises are particularly painful for cats. And that's what inspires their fear.

Fear of loud noises is another survival tool for cats. If a little noise is a signal that something to eat might be nearby, then a very loud noise acts the same as a fire alarm held up next to their ears. And that means DANGER. And that means FIGHT or RUN AWAY.

When a cat is frightened, running away or hiding is a common response. But sometimes if a cat feels trapped or cornered, she'll stand still while unusual things happen to her body.

First, all of the fur on her body will stand on end. Then the cat will arch her back up using all sixty of her vertebrae—humans have only thirty-four, by the way. This will make the cat look much bigger; a tactic it uses to intimidate its enemies. But the sign to be very aware of is when a cat has turned its ears back. A cat will do this when it feels like fighting back and wants to protect those sensitive ears. That is a clear sign to back away from a VERY angry cat that could attack you.

Never mind all that ear stuff! I gotta go grab that cat!

Here,
Kitty,
Kitty,
Kitty!

•CHAPTER FIVE•
CATCH THAT KITTY

*Hark!

MEANWHILE, IN THE SECRET BASEMENT LAIR OF STRANGE KITTY . . .

DO YOU HEAR THAT, OLD CHUM? I DO BELIEVE I HEAR PLAINTIVE CRIES FOR HELP FROM OUR OLD FELINE FRIEND WITH THE BLACK FUR AND REBELLIOUS ATTITUDE!

HOLY CATNIP, S.K.! WE CAN'T IGNORE A PLAINTIVE CRY FOR HELP!

RIGHT YOU ARE, OLD BEAN! ONCE AGAIN, THE WORLD IS IN NEED OF . . .

OKAY . . . LET'S
SEE HERE . . .

COOL UTILITY
BELT?

YUP!

SUPER COOL MYSTICAL
CAPE OF NINJA
STEALTH?

YUP!

SUPER, HYPER COOL
FLASHLIGHT
WITH
COPYRIGHT-
PROTECTED
LOGO TAPED
ON IT?

YUP!

SPATULA?

YUP!

HOW ABOUT . . .
"UP, UP, AND AWAY!"

IT'S BEEN DONE.

"ON YOUR MARK, GET SET, GO!"

IT DOESN'T FEEL QUITE RIGHT.

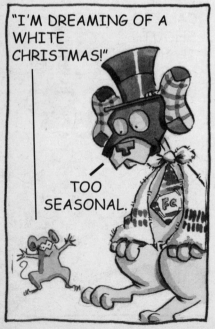

"I'M DREAMING OF A WHITE CHRISTMAS!"

TOO SEASONAL.

CHEESE POPCORN?

HMMM . . . WILL IT REALLY STRIKE FEAR IN THE HEARTS OF OUR MOST BITTER AND DANGEROUS ENEMIES?

NO ... I MEAN ...
I'M GOING TO MAKE
SOME CHEESE
POPCORN. DO
YOU WANT
SOME?

OH, I SEE.
YES, PLEASE.

WAIT! I'VE
GOT IT!

REALLY?

LOOK OUT FOR
THE SPATULA!

I LOVE IT!

OH, GOOD! THEN
IT'S SETTLED ...

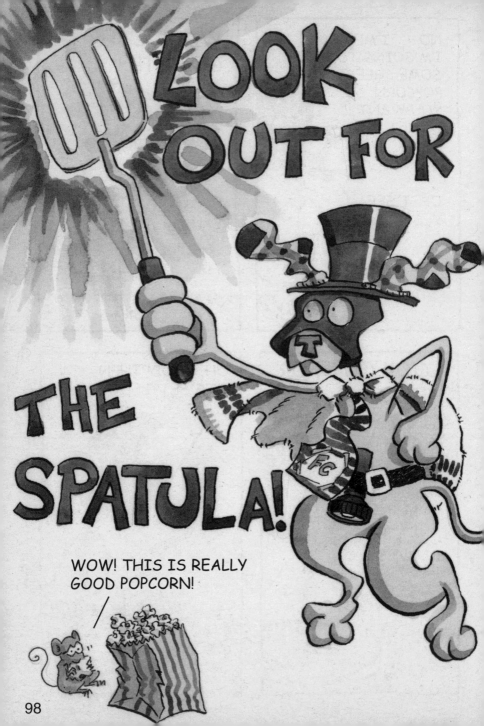

LOOK OUT FOR THE SPATULA!

WOW! THIS IS REALLY GOOD POPCORN!

•CHAPTER SIX•

KITTIES TO
THE RESCUE

SLAM!

Well . . . at least I got her back in the house.

108

*Let us in, and I mean RIGHT MEOW!

RIGHT
NOW!!

MEOW*
MEOW*

*Get ME OUT of here!

That's right! You heard me! As soon as I open this door, I'll be free. FREE! No more goofy cats screaming in my face and eating my shoes. No more biting and scratching and chasing me down the street. Outside this door is a big, wonderful world where goofy cats don't turn into furry whirl-winds that hit me on the head with a spatula. And soon I will be a part of that world once again!

YAWN

•CHAPTER SEVEN•
KITTY ON HER OWN

133

MEOW?

WHY ARE SOME CATS AFRAID OF BEING ALONE?

MEOW?

Cats are independent animals. There's no question about that. They're very good at taking care of themselves in the wild. But when cats have become house cats, they usually become "bonded" with their owner.

When a cat becomes very close, even dependent on a human being for food or protection, that's called "bonding."

And sometimes when that bond is broken, even for just a little while, some cats might exhibit "separation anxiety." Have you ever seen a baby begin to cry just because her Mommy has left the room for just a few seconds? That's a good example of "separation anxiety," and even cats can get it.

Leave cats alone for too long and they'll start to cry out to see if anyone is in the house, just like a baby. Sometimes they'll even lose their appetite and not eat. The most anxious cats will even pull out clumps of their own fur because of nervousness.

The solution for all fears is to let the cat gradually grow used to whatever scares them. Cats can adapt very quickly.

If a cat is afraid of people, keep your distance and step a little closer day by day while also letting her come to you under her own power. If your cat is afraid of loud noises, try to keep the sound down at first if possible, and then increase the exposure a little bit each day.

And if the cat is afraid of being alone, give her time to adjust as she learns that you'll eventually return. She'll hate being alone at first, but in time she'll learn that there's nothing to be afraid of once you keep coming back.

138

So, let's you and me make a deal, cat. We're going to be stuck together for the next few days. I'm going to feed you and take good care of you no matter what.

And in return . . . how about you be just a little nicer to me.

144

MEOW
CRASH
BLAM
WOOF
Although . . . something tells me this is STILL going to be a very long week.
THUMP
ARF
HISS
ZAP
KA-BOOM
DING
SPLAT

• EPILOGUE •

148

Thank you so much, Uncle Murray, for taking such good care of Kitty and Puppy. I know they can be a real handful. I hope they weren't too much trouble.

Fish.

What did you say, Uncle Murray?

Fish don't bite or scream or chase you around the house or hit you on the head with a spatula. All they do is swim around and make nice little bubbles that don't hurt anybody. And they're pretty. Pretty like little rainbows. Fish.

Fish don't bite or scream or chase you around the house or . . .

Hmmm . . . Oh, well. Goodbye, Uncle Murray. And thanks again.

HI, KITTY!
Did you miss us?

Awwww! We missed you, too, Kitty!

HEY! Do you remember that REAL BIG SURPRISE we promised you? Do you? DO YOU?!

Well, here she is!

To be continued in . . .

BAD KITTY
HAS A BABY

• APPENDIX •

A SELECTION OF PHOBIAS

A "phobia" is a strong fear of a specific object or a specific situation. Most of the time the fear is irrational, meaning that the person who has the phobia really has nothing to fear. For instance, a boy might be afraid of worms (Scoleciphobia), but that doesn't mean the boy has any real reason to be afraid of worms, other than he thinks they're scary and doesn't want them anywhere near him.

Ten percent of the people who live in the United States have a phobia. That's over thirty million people! This means that phobias are very common and nothing to be ashamed of.

We've seen a lot of different examples of fear in this book. The following is a small selection of the more than five hundred known phobias.

Agrizoophobia—Fear of wild animals.

Ailurophobia (also, Elurophobia)—Fear of cats.

Amychophobia—Fear of scratches or being scratched.

Cynophobia—Fear of dogs.

Ligyrophobia (also, Phonophobia)—Fear of loud noises, also, fear of voices or one's own voice.

Lilapsophobia—Fear of hurricanes or tornadoes.

Monophobia (also Autophobia)—Fear of being alone.

Olfactophobia (also, Osmophobia)—Fear of smells or odors.

Peladophobia—Fear of bald people.

Phagophobia—Fear of swallowing, eating, or being eaten.

Pnigophobia—Fear of being choked or smothered.

Teratophobia—Fear of monsters.

NICK BRUEL has written and illustrated some pretty funny books, including *Poor Puppy, Boing, Bob and Otto, Little Red Bird*, and *Who is Melvin Bubble?*, winner of the North Carolina Children's Choice Award. HOWEVER, he is probably best known as the author of the Tennessee, Wyoming, and Indiana Children's Choice Award winner *Bad Kitty* (available in regular and special Cat-Nipped editions), about which some very important people said:

★"Perhaps the hammiest, most expressive feline ever captured in watercolors."
—*Kirkus Reviews*, starred review

★"Will have youngsters howling with laughter."
—*Publishers Weekly*, starred review

He is also infamous for his Bad Kitty chapter books, *Bad Kitty Gets a Bath* (winner of a 2009 Gryphon Honor), and *Happy Birthday, Bad Kitty*. Visit him online at www.nickbruel.com.